PADDY DOG sees a GHOST

BY JUNE WOODMAN

ILLUSTRATED BY PAMELA STOREY

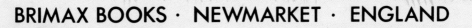

BRIMAX BOOKS · NEWMARKET · ENGLAND

Paddy Dog is in his little house. It is a very windy day. Paddy looks out of the window. He sees the leaves falling off the trees.
"It is a good day for doing some washing," he says. Paddy Dog likes to be clean.

Paddy goes to get all his
dirty washing.
"My sheets are dirty," he says,
"and my pillow case too."
Paddy takes the table cloth.
He takes his scarf and his
dirty socks. He puts all the
dirty things into the wash tub.

Then Paddy Dog fills the wash
tub with very hot water.
He puts in lots of soap powder.
Then he rubs and he scrubs
until his things are clean.
Paddy goes outside to hang
the clean things on the line.
The wind is blowing hard.

"Now I will go and see Dilly
Duck," says Paddy Dog.
He goes to the duck pond.
Dilly is washing her three
little ducklings.
"It is a good day for doing
washing," says Paddy Dog.
"You are silly!" says Dilly.
"The wind is blowing too hard.
Look! All your washing is
blowing away."

"Oh no!" says Paddy Dog. He runs down the lane after his washing. He finds his socks in the hedge. He finds his table cloth on a bush. Flippy Frog finds the scarf and pillow case. They are in the pond.

Poor Paddy Dog.
His washing is all dirty.
He cannot find his sheet.
It is not in the hedge.
It is not in the bush.
It is not by the duck pond.
Is it in the forest?

It is very dark in the forest.
Paddy Dog is afraid.
Something goes "Hoo-hoo-hoo!"
Paddy sees something white.
It is up in the tree.
"A ghost!" says Paddy Dog.
He is not very brave.
Paddy Dog runs away fast.

Paddy runs to Hoppy Rabbit's
house. Hoppy is outside,
washing his little car.
He rubs and he scrubs until
it is clean.
"There is a ghost in the
forest!" says Paddy.
"No," says Hoppy Rabbit.
"Yes," says Paddy. "It is up
in the tree."
"Let us tell Bossy Bear,"
says Hoppy Rabbit.

They run to Bossy Bear's
house. Bossy is outside,
washing the windows.
He rubs and he scrubs until
they are clean.
"There is a ghost in the
forest!" say Hoppy and Paddy.
"No," says Bossy.
"Yes," say Hoppy and Paddy.
"It is up in the tree."
"Let us tell Dilly Duck,"
says Bossy.

Dilly and her ducklings are by the duck pond. Merry Mole and Flippy Frog are there too. "There is a ghost in the forest!" say Paddy and Hoppy and Bossy.
"You are silly!" says Dilly.
"Come and see," says Paddy Dog.

So they all go to the forest.
They are afraid, but they
try to be brave.
Then they see something
white in the tree.
"Hoo-hoo-hoo!" it goes.
They all hear it.
"It is a ghost!" says Dilly.
They are not brave at all.
They run away.

Then Cuddly Cat comes by.
She sees something white.
"Hoo-hoo-hoo!" it goes.
"What is that?" says Cuddly.
"It is a ghost in the tree,"
says Paddy Dog.
"I will go and see," says
Cuddly Cat.
"Look out!" says Hoppy.
"The ghost will get you!"

But Cuddly is very brave.
She goes up in the tree.
She lifts up part of the sheet.
"Hoo-hoo-hoo!"
"Look!" says Cuddly Cat.
They all shout,
"We know you!"
It is not a ghost.
It is Ozzie Owl!

Say these words again

windy

blowing

washing

window

outside

clean

shout

pillow

soap powder

something